Undue Respect

By Oliver S. Carter

*"I understand everything is connected, that all roads
meet, and that all rivers flow into the same sea." —Paulo Coelho*

COLOURED PDF VERSION

For Nicole.

Character List:

Primary Characters

LORD JOHN ASHLEY (mid-20s): Silver-tongued nobleman in debt to The Savoy Hotel.

BETTY ACTON (mid-20s): Impoverished shopkeep, left to care for her little sister.

BERT MACAVOY (late-50s): Owner of The Savoy Hotel and pioneer of lever watches.

DELLA DUKE (late-20s): Prostitute on a mission to find true love.

Secondary Characters

Otto Schenk: Lord John's butler.

Earl Francis "Fritz" Ashley: Lord John's father.

Kate Acton: Betty's little sister.

Tertiary Characters

William Acton: Betty and Kate's father.

Viscount Ashley: Lord John's brother.

Mrs MacAvoy: Bert MacAvoy's wife and William Acton's love affair.

Prologue

'I'd like to share a story with you about four strangers — a wayward nobleman, a thieving capitalist, a starving shopkeep, and a yearning prostitute — whose lives became intertwined in the most unexpected of ways.'

The shop was saturated with the scent of cedarwood, but every time the door swung open, bringing in a gust of English summer air, the smell of hollyhocks from a nearby garden would drift in with it. The rustling of leaves in the wind drowned out the sound of carriages and the rumble of iron-shod hooves on cobblestone streets below. The weathervanes moved back and forth in their cages like spectators at a tennis match, for they did not like being confined. The wind blew through the great beech trees, prompting their branches to reach toward the glass casing that separated them from the inside, only just touching the glass.

The inside was full of a jumble of transparent cases hanging from threads and wires and chains, each one holding a variety of different hats. Some were bonnets, some bowlers, some gamblers, and some homburgs. All were filled with dust that kept

them from sparkling in their cases and showed they had been
sitting there for ages. A narrow foyer between W. Acton Hat and
Dress Shoppe and the Acton residence was decorated with
dilapidated paintings, puny marble sculptures, and a matte mirror
in a plain bronze frame. It was also occupied by Betty Acton,
whose slight nose, and cheeks, suffused with a divine blush, did
well to entice willing customers. Hunched over the display case of
hats, she rested her elbow upon the glass. And as potential
shoppers passed, the curls on her head would scatter haphazardly,
leaving smudges behind (a medium ideal for illustrating tedium). A
young girl — her sister, about twelve — stood to her left. She, too,
had black ringlets and rosy cheeks but was smaller than the
woman. And she was scowling at the store window, on the cusp of
being too young to be scowling at anything.

Betty looked over at Kate and sighed sadly. 'It looks as
though we won't be having supper tonight,' she remarked. 'Unless
someone comes in at this odd hour.' And although the bell above
the door was quiet, they heard the distinctive buoyant stride of
English nobility as Lord John Ashley entered the room. A
secondary heir to Earl Francis Ashley and brother to Viscount
Ashley, Lord John had porcelain skin that showcased his soft, pink
mouth, guarded by his debonair, coffee-coloured moustache. And

although he stood no taller than 5'5", his individual constitution was full of charm and enchantment (that is, until you got to know him).

'Good evening,' the man said to the woman behind the counter. 'Are you by chance selling any newsboy caps?' He was dressed like a classically-styled Londoner.

'Newsboy caps?' Betty asked. 'You, sir, want a nicer hat than a newsboy cap, something with more style. Let me see, how about this belled top hat? Yes, that's the one.'

'A newsboy cap is just fine, thank you.' She reluctantly pulled out two hats: one light grey and one dark; he picked the dark one.

'That will be... 20 pence,' Betty announced, breathing a sigh of relief. Lord John Ashley paid, nodded, and gave her a polite goodbye before exiting the building, careful to dodge the vicious beech trees, which struck him anyways. He mounted his matching dark grey horse outside and rode up Station Road.

Upon arriving at The Savoy Hotel, Lord John set down his suit jacket, dismounted from his horse, and tossed a single pence to one of the raggedy street urchins lingering by the gates. The intricate and boxy shape of the building dwarfed the tiny bellboys, the grandeur of its aesthetic glory making other nearby buildings look inferior by comparison. Each night, the domes on the roof — because of their rounded shape — rinsed themselves of any grime when it rained, so they would be gleaming again in the morning, and the view of the Thames River upon which the dome shone was one that would be captured on canvas for centuries to come.

The inside of The Savoy was equally dazzling. Doric columns were believed to have been stolen from the Colosseum and topped off with golden leaves purportedly plucked straight from the Garden of Eden. The floor was red, so red it almost seemed to be on fire, and the walls were a yellowy-white colour that illuminated a soft, warm lustre. It never got old; no one had ever seen anything like it before. Everyone who visited the building with the rich red floor knew its value and acted accordingly. All but one Lord John Ashley, who now donned unfashionably torn trousers and a white undershirt, so as to masquerade as anyone but himself. He was also the only one to wear a newsboy cap, although it was backwards and so framed his face to make him thicker around the cheeks. He made his way to Room 131.

A man whose hair resembled a rat's nest left the room with a guilty grin on his face. He did not change his expression as he passed by Lord John, who knocked on the white door, which swung open at once.

'You're here for your appointment?' a young lady asked. The woman smiled devilishly in front of him, knowing full well who he was and what he wanted. The light was dim, but her features were still visible. She had an ugly face but an incredible body and had probably been told many times how gorgeous she was, although she did not look like she believed it. Her name was Della Duke; she was a "man-pleaser" and respected artist of promiscuity.

'Good day, Della.'

'Johnny-Boy, darling, you know you mustn't be running around in clothes like these, looking like a beggar!'

'That's awfully charming coming from you. You — more than anyone — know I cannot be recognized in these quarters, Della. Especially not when MacAvoy is around; he's already got me in enough debt!'

'You must be paying them off if you have money left over to pay me,' she joked, knowing full well Lord John was far from it. 'Now shut up and kiss me.'

As the two made love, the hotel owner, pioneer of lever watches, and most well-respected investor in all of London, Bert

MacAvoy, made his way through the hallways just outside, his neatly polished shoes clicking across the floor. He was a plump fellow but carried himself like a king. His curly ginger hair, spotted with strings of white, created the outline of a circle around his largely bald head, but it was ultimately his bright cherubic face that competed with the floor for reddest in colour. He cruised the silken floors and summoned butlers and hotel staff alike at the clap of his hands. As he exited the hotel, he entered his carriage. The horses trotted, and he sat down with a gasp — his belly fat swayed like water in a wheelbarrow. Monocle to his eye, he started on the latest issue of *The Times*, just barely making out the letters in the darkness of the night.

Reading an article entitled LEVER WATCHES SKYROCKET IN SALES, MacAvoy's head popped up from behind the newspaper to see his homely, spruce mansion. He was pleased to see that his wife was safe at home. However, when he entered the house, he heard a loud clatter coming from upstairs, comparable to the familiar sound of horses' hooves. At first, he thought there were two horses in his room, but he was shocked to find they were replaced by two much less sensible animals: a man and MacAvoy's wife, who was completely naked.

'William Acton?!' he trembled. His face grew redder and redder as he ran to his broomstick and chased the naked man, wearing nothing but a hat, downstairs and out into the night. All of London was asleep by now, and William, a slender fellow with a peculiar upper lip and black, curled hair, darted home to W. Acton Hat and Dress Shoppe.

'Father, tell me why you're holding a homburg to your... homburg,' his daughter, Betty Acton asked, mortified, in the dim light of the store at night. The wind howled and the trees continued to swipe the remarkably resilient glass hat and dress shop. William held the hat in his hands while looking out onto the street. He returned to his bedroom and sat on his bed, unable to stand due to the overwhelming smell of cedarwood.

Part 1

Chapter 1

The Nobleman

'Otto, fetch me a wine, will you?'

'Yes, my lord.'

Lord John Ashley was known for many things in London: nobility, conman, thief, liar, patron of brothels, and most notably: ignoring the noble traditions of his father Earl Francis Ashley and embarrassing the family. A ripple of whispers always followed him because of his differences from the other aristocrats.

'Ottfried, friend, tell me: how is my father?' said Lord John, reading the paper and laying flat upon a divan sofa, his elbow resting on a pillow next to a bowl of fruit. Lord John lived in the manor house of Totten Hall — just upon Tottenham Court Road — whose narrow stretches of stairs and whimsical architecture made it better known as the Totten Labyrinth.

'He is increasingly unwell, my lord,' said Otto. The peculiarly hairy German butler grabbed an imported bottle of wine and a stemmed glass. He picked up a white cloth napkin and poured the wine into the glass, but splashed a drop of it across the silver cup. 'Scheiße!' he said to himself.

'Marvellous,' Lord John replied. 'And have you been able to get your hands on his will yet?'

'No, my lord.'

'Hasten up, then,' John John demanded, proceeding to flick his tongue across his thumb to turn the page of the paper to page six. The rationale behind this idea was simple: Lord John, having been disinherited by his father, would be entitled to a portion of his father's estate under English common law had a will not been drawn in the first place.

'Yes, my lord.'

'Otto, tell me about this wedding ball my brother is throwing on Friday,' Lord John said, holding his wine glass and swirling the red liquid around a bit before drinking.

'Well, my lord, there is a ball on Friday, held in honour of your brother Viscount Ashley's wedding and Jane Crawley of Sussex, and–'

'I've always found balls too ostentatious, too showy. Amorous young men outnumber ladies, whose primary desire is to dance, and, mind you, not upon the sweaty bodies of bare boys. The music may as well be strummed by a lowly band of kiddy-fiddlers — that is, dear Otto, to say fiddlers who are children. And frankly, the dancing should come *before* food is served, in the same manner that socks come *before* shoes, wealth *before* health, scrumping *before* marriage.'

'Heresy, my lord.'

'Even a more righteous clergy member wouldn't mind a good scrumping from time to time, Otto. Look no further than the band,' Lord John spat. Then he was snorting, chuckling at his own laughter. 'All of this is to say that, despite my contempt towards balls, I will indulge nonetheless.' He arose from the divan and wiped his suit jacket with his hands so as to clean it. Then, while holding the Merlot-filled glass by its stem, he walked over to the sink and emptied the wine down the drain, and the reddish-brown liquid stained the perimeter of the sink.

Despite the lavish life he lived, Lord John was in substantial debt to several, most notably Bert MacAvoy, for a series of overstay charges at The Savoy, amounting to an impressive £214.00. He had always known what type of life he was meant to live. The lights of The Savoy danced before his mind's eye and reminded him that his ambition would one day be realised-if only he could earn enough money to pay off his debts and settle down like his father once did and his brother is now doing.

'Otto, dear brother,' Lord John began. 'Have you any qualms with the ultimate ceremony of love?'

'Do you mean to refer to copulation, my lord?'

'Well, yes, but no,' said Lord John, with no apparent reason to protest. 'I mean to reference the event of love which is marriage.

Don't you think it's all quite... theatrical? Don't you think it was invented by those who see love as something to be sold? Love is like any other commodity. Its participants are like market clientele, and they are stimulated by love in the same way that others are stimulated by consumer goods. *And how the market is stimulated by love*: tiny clothes, upstarts, grandiose weddings, *compromise*! Such are the fundamentals of laissez-faire — as I was educated in at Oxford, mind you. It's all a game of power, prestige, and status. Is this what we should be playing with? I don't know. And it doesn't help that love is so impossible to explain... We are trying to invent a definition of something that has been tried to be defined by so many others. Deep down in the pit of my stomach, I cannot help but feel that it is all a game like any other. But what a game! Perhaps one day the answer will be clear. But until then, I must end my soliloquy empty-handed.' His frown grew wretched and his brows knitted. 'Oh, and while you're pondering this, could you fetch me a turnover?'

'You seem, my lord, to speak of love with the parlance of a stockbroker,' said Otto, 'and while I am not in the least equipped with the knowledge or experience to answer your questions — strawberry or blueberry, my lord? — I do know that even stockbrokers grow affectionate for their trade.'

'Yes, yes — blueberry, please — perhaps the apex of my love life is Della,' Lord John Ashley said, outwardly trembling at the thought of it. 'Agh, bugger all!' Lord John glanced down at Otto and then turned towards the door, next to which he had been standing like a sentinel for the last several minutes. Starting for the door, Lord John turned the knob and ran out into the street.

'Strike me once or strike me ten times! I will not know the difference once I have been stricken initial!' He weaved in and out of traffic, and horses and their respective carriages soon swerved around him, occasionally bumping into the smaller vehicle that was his body. Otto, not fully unacquainted with this behaviour and rather amused, watched.

Chapter 2

The Capitalist

Bert MacAvoy shouted from The Savoy's upper floor balustrades, 'Get a move on!' His face was red with rage after a series of 'issues' concerning his wife and William Acton. The following day was the ball he wanted no part of. 'It's tomorrow, you fools!'

MacAvoy wasn't always like this. Born and raised on a cattle farm in Ipswich, the youngin learned to stand as soon as his legs could support him. When he was three months old, the boy learned to walk. By the time he was a year old, he learned to run, and when he was three years old he learned to swim. His mother was never able to keep up with him. Cows were still new to the boy when he was four years old, but it took not long for MacAvoy to figure out how to milk them and tend their wounds. He got along well with his fellow youngins, too. They all liked his stories of wandering through the pastures and feeding the geese that waddled around there. They liked his sense of humour and his tendency to laugh at any joke. Some say his strength and maturity was due to of the cow milk that made his bones so strong and his head screwed on so right. Others say it was the steak, full of red and white bovine blood.

By the time he turned six, MacAvoy took to selling his father's cows to traders from Essex and Norfolk, who came every other Tuesday to Ipswich and asked him "How much?" in a thick accent as he stood by their supplies with his Beaumont-Adams revolver strapped to his hip. He began to eat potatoes nearly every day with more gravy than any two men combined could hold. His taste buds had been moulded on potatoes, their smooth round shapes, their starchy bulk, their cool slickness — so different from tender meat and the sharp, metallic flavour of vegetables like broccoli or string beans. However, the young lad suffered the consequences of his diet at school, disdained and derided by his peers. He sneered back at them in the hallways and followed their movements with his eyes. He was determined to show them all that they were nothing to him and never would be.

At age thirteen, young MacAvoy was enrolled in a multitude of classes: art history, religion, maths, physics, chemistry, biology, Latin, English, physical education, architecture, and philosophy. He was soon admitted into Oxford University on his own merits and swiftly ascended the ranks. He arrived eager and enthusiastic to learn and was recognized by his peers as an expert in the field of engineering. However, the young man soon grew resentful of them, as they delighted in mockery against MacAvoy like they once did long ago. One known by the name of Fritz, better known now as Earl Francis Ashley — Lord John Ashley's father — was particularly cruel. The handsome, slender boy with thin lips and bright eyes was hardly kind to the lumbering young man, who moved in much more of a rolling gait than a walk. Several times he would comment on how slow MacAvoy was and how he would never live up to his father's expectations.

On one ordinary day, the sun had risen above the eastern line and its bright yellow light spilt through the window into the buildings. Bees and golden flies hovered around each flower, and people emerged from their houses to work. Through the window of Fritz's dormitory, MacAvoy peered into the room. Bent at a strange angle, he reached in with his broomstick-like hand and found his term project upon his desk: the world's first lever watch. Assigned in a task to design an improved clock, the gadget ticked with a smooth yet complex rhythm that was unlike any other watch currently on the market. The brass case that housed it glowed brightly in the sunlight and the hands of the watch spun slowly as it sliced through space. MacAvoy copied down the details of the manual in his own handwriting, snatched the watch, and passed it off as his own.

Needless to say, MacAvoy had turned from an indebted student to a wealthy investor and eventual hotel connoisseur in a matter of days. After all, its creator, Earl Francis Ashley, had larger duties at hand now and all responsibilities regarding the watch were diminished in his mind. He had imagined that once the watch was made, his work was over, never to work on the watch again. Indeed, his wealth was already so great that a civil suit would hardly have even made a difference.

MacAvoy had been thinking for decades about what to do with all the wealth he had accumulated from his brief episode of theft which supported his exorbitant lifestyle. He was since surrounded by women eager to marry him, one of whom he settled on. He had visions for what he wanted to do with his money; most notably, he wanted to found a hotel. His original vision for The Savoy was to create a hotel with a modern feel that would appeal to more than just Englishmen on holiday. His belief was that he could take the grandeur of European hotels and combine it with the luxury of American hotels. This would produce something grander and more spacious than anything that had ever been constructed during his lifetime. At the same time, he believed he could take advantage of the continent's more relaxed attitude to human existence: an attitude that, though it might inspire dissatisfaction in those who had to struggle for every scrap of pleasure in their lives, was nevertheless ripe with possibility to those naturally content with life. He believed he could blend these ideas and create an experience that would be magical for his guests, even if it couldn't completely erase the sour taste left in his mouth by his own unhappy childhood and adolescence, which brings us to the present day.

MacAvoy shouted and screeched at the staff, sweat pouring down his face. His eyes were white and his face was grotesque and terrifying. The veins on his neck stood out like ropes and his mouth was a snarling hole. 'I've told you lot over and over and over again, I don't know how many times! You made thousands of these tables and you can't even put one together right!' he finished screaming at the staff. They sat in shock, their faces drained of colour, their eyes wide with fear. Bert MacAvoy had a short temper and was never, ever satisfied with any work his employees did. Indeed, Bert MacAvoy was never satisfied with anything.

Chapter 3

The Shopkeep

The piece of paper flew like a kite, its edges already blackened by the rain. With only one corner, clung to the glass wall of the hat and dress shop.

'Oi twat, has your mother taught you not to stick flyers to the glass?!' Betty Acton yelled after the boy who had hung it, waving her fist. He glanced back, then walked away and out into the rain again. Betty reached for the bin and gave the flyer a look.

ROYAL WEDDING BALL

of VISCOUNT PIERS ASHLEY and JANE CRAWLEY of SUSSEX

FRIDAY, 25 May at THE SAVOY HOTEL

DRESS ACCORDINGLY

How she dreamed of being a part of the London upper crust. In a regretful sigh, she turned her body towards Kate, who was sitting in the corner of the room at a low table with oil pastels. Their mother had died of the flu or smallpox or something of the sort; they couldn't afford medical help to tell them one way or the other. And as for their father: while he wasn't secretly off with Mrs MacAvoy, he was home drunk most of the time. Even if their father had been there to care for Kate, Betty wouldn't have had the resources to go to the ball. So she tossed the flyer.

The hat and dress shop was quiet, still. It sat between an apothecary and a bakery. A blue awning had been stretched across the entrance, and the letters on the tinted windows were mirrored, so you couldn't read them from the outside. But Betty knew what was in those windows. She stacked the hats on the shelves in those windows, and sometimes during the slow hours, she would look in them and imagine she was wearing them.

There was a black one with a wide brim, made from fine felt, with a small black feather hanging from a clip on the back, that matched the black laced dress just right of it perfectly. A peacock feather hat with a large turquoise feather curving over it was also one of her favourites to look at. There was a wide-brimmed white hat, trimmed with pink ombre fabric and small pearls at the base of the brim, that looked like it would be fun to wear outside on a sunny day.

The dresses were equally stunning. One dress was strapless and had a corset-style waistline. It had a small row of pearls down the centre of the dress, and a long, flowing skirt. It was beautiful, but she preferred dresses with sleeves because they didn't get in the way when she did things. There was another dress she liked that had black sleeves and a very full white skirt but no corset or bodice. The skirt fell in large folds around her knees, shortening her legs by about a foot. But one dress was especially charming to her: it was blue and covered her wrists, bodice and skirt in billowing folds of cloth. It was like a piece of the sky had been sewn into a dress and gifted to her. However, this was not her wardrobe; it was a shop, and these were not hers to wear.

Betty Acton's afternoons usually consisted of a series of waiting; that is, if one were to remove the odd conversations with Kate or last-minute requests to purchase an old hat. She was nothing if not flexible. On the infrequent occasion that a potential buyer was interested in the hats or dresses, she would greet them with:

'Enjoying the afternoon?'

'Quite,' a peculiarly hairy man replied, bowing. 'Otto Schenk, pleasure.'

'An introduction — how very... formal. Betty Acton; it is a pleasure to meet you as well, Otto.' The man wandered around the hat section of the shop, in search of the perfect hat for his lord, John Ashley.

'Anticipating the ball?' Otto asked.

'I'll be working.'

'Ah, bullocks! It's not every day that one gets to attend a viscount's wedding ball,' Otto replied. 'You should be enjoying yourself, not worrying about work. Let your hair down and have some fun. The music is playing, the champagne is flowing, and the most eligible bachelors in all of England are there.' There was a long pause following Otto's words.

'Is there anything, in particular, you are looking for?'

'A hat.' Otto carefully analysed each of the hats, discarding the ones that wouldn't be appropriate for Lord John's garb. The German settled on a homburg, naturally.

'One homburg?' Betty asked.

Otto smiled, bobbing his head to the side as if he were a bird. 'Yes, miss.' He shifted his feet and she sorted the change. 'Lovely dresses you've got here. Ladies must be rushing to get them in time for the wedding ball.' A rat scurried across the floor and under a dresser, narrowly avoiding Otto's toes. The change was evenly distributed into his cupped hands, and he let it slip between his fingers back into her hand. He left, but his words resonated with her. The whips of poverty stung too deeply for far too long, and for just one night she wanted to be swept up in her own fairy tale. She refused to let the waiting resume.

Chapter 4

The Prostitute

Della Cassandra Duke wanted nothing more in the world than to be loved.

'Oh, darling – tell me about your passions, your dreams, all which you have to say and all which you choose not to!' she would beg of her clients. As a little girl, she had grown up without a father, but she grew up to have phenomenal success as a dominatrix. 'You have revealed yourself to me physically, dearest. *Now reveal yourself to me emotionally!*' Her body was a gorgeous hourglass – thin shoulders, moderate breasts and a waist that no other woman could match. But her face did not come close to matching the beauty of her figure: her nose swung to one side or the other depending on the time of day; her lips were crusted with skin; and her teeth – what a horrible arrangement of enamel and dentin God so deviously devised.

Della was happy in her work, but she had to admit some sadness about the path she had chosen. Her first career choice, made as an idealistic sixteen-year-old, had been a school teacher. She had even worked her way through college and pursued a career in teaching, but after four years of working three part-time jobs just to keep body and soul together, she had grown disillusioned by the realities of the profession. No woman made a living doing what she loved. The night she walked into the bar, thinking she had hit rock bottom, she'd discovered gold. Men flocked her for her fabulous figure, and she found mighty success in this arena. With each paycheque, her despair lifted like a bank cloud from the horizon of her mind. She allowed herself the indulgence of luxury and jewellery and fine clothing. And a blooming desire for more had arisen, and her demands — in regard to love — became taller.

On the day of the ball, just outside of The Savoy, the sun hung like a bronze coin, nestled among a string of clouds the colour of plums. Della Duke opened her handbag and pulled out a box of cigarettes with one hand and a small, silver lighter in the other. She struck the lighter and brought it up to her mouth, tilting her head back and inhaling deeply as she shut her eyes. The motionless air in front of her face rippled with heat as she exhaled three perfect smoke rings. Wide-eyed boys sitting with their mothers on park benches stared at the rings as they crossed the sky.

The Earl and his son, Viscount Ashley, were in a huddle nearby, scouting the area for tonight's event. As the viscount ascended into the mahogany double doors of the establishment, escorted by MacAvoy who was frequently checked his lever watch, his father stood outside aimlessly.

'Planning to attend the ball?' he asked Della, trying to start up a conversation with the prostitute.

'Not particularly,' answered Della Duke, unconcerned about his status. They both sat in the thick silence of the deserted streets for a moment. She pulled on her cigarette and turned to him halfway. 'And you?'

'Dear girl, do you think I can dance at my age?' he replied, answering her question with a question. 'I have been unwell for quite some time now.' After another short pause came a request from the married earl. 'However, if you would like to visit Spencer House tonight, just upon St. James's Place, I would be delighted to speak with you then? Perhaps we could have a chat.'

'That sounds pleasant. I do quite fancy a chat, Earl Francis Ashley.'

'Ah, you know who I am. But please, madam, the name is Fritz to you.

Part 2

Chapter 5

The Savoy

The time had finally come. Englishmen and women flocked the rich red floors of The Savoy to dance. They filled the space with the sounds of their laughter and the scent of their rosy perfume and musky cologne. Women, attired in satin gowns with glittering jewels, swung in the arms of their suitors, new and old, in a swirling sea of blue and red and yellow uniforms, while graceful Englishwomen strolled by in beaded dresses, their high heels clicking on the oak floors like hard rain on a tin roof. Here the walls were draped in Satin, and a festive illumination of oil lamps bathed the rooms in light that turned to scented smoke. The room was alight and alive. It was the season of masked balls and gorgeous costumes, of gambling and gossip, of laughter and flirtation and tenderness. There was no place to be but here, on these gilded floors, watching girls in rich satins spin past in jewels that sparkled in the light from electric chandeliers; boys who puffed on cigarettes as they walked arm-in-arm with dainty English girls from good families.

Betty Acton entered, dressed in her favourite sky blue bodice and skirt in billowing folds of cloth stolen from the shop. And while this was certainly a severe breach of her father's rules and an act that ought not to be committed, he would hardly have noticed anyways. She could not help but marvel at what seemed to be a never-ending sea of people, all dressed for pleasure and uninhibited amusement. Their clothes were brighter than the rainbow. Their smiles were wider than the sun. A juggler tossed balls of coloured light into the air, and all around him people caught the sparkles, held them for a moment, then let them go in favour of the next. The laughter was like the peal of silver bells. Some people danced, others ate biscuits and doughnuts that dripped with honey, and still, others paused to rest their tired feet. Betty took a plate piled with sugary sweets and ate some tea cakes before returning to her sister Kate, dressed in a frilly pink dress with a huge bow at the neck.

Her plan was simple: she'd pass by the men as they ranked their whisky and nudged each other and talked loudly. They wouldn't notice the short, full-figured woman in the blue dress. She'd smile at them and bat her eyes and saunter past, digging into their pockets while they were distracted by Kate, then stuffing her brassiere with loose change as hard as she could (as if it were a balloon about to pop) until she was satisfied.

'Pardon, sir,' Kate would say. 'Do you know where I could find the powder room?' Answers flooded in as the night progressed.

'Ah, yes,' the first man said. 'It's right down the corner.'

'Oh, just turn at the foyer,' the second man suggested.

'I couldn't tell you, my dear,' the third said. 'I just got here myself.'

The fourth man shook his head. 'Perhaps you should ask my wife. She knows this place better than I do'

'Listen, if you ask me,' the fifth man replied, 'I would start by asking one of the servers. Those guys know all the secrets of this place. They practically live here. They might know where it is. I don't have a clue myself, though. Sorry!'

Regardless of their answer, money started pouring in as Betty swiped infinite coins from these unsuspecting noblemen. The coins appeared as if by magic, as if a fairy had formed them out of the ether. And as soon as they started flooding her brassiere, Betty casually clutched the stack and dumped it into her purse, which grew larger and larger. The noblemen still didn't notice.

'Pardon, sir,' Kate would say. 'Do you know where I could find the powder room?'

A man with porcelain skin that showcased his soft, pink mouth, guarded by his debonair, coffee-coloured moustache, turned around.

'The powder room?'

'Yes, sir, the powder room.' And just as Lord John Ashley started to speak, he felt the gentle pull of something from his back pocket. Certainly, no pickpockets were in attendance at the ball, he thought. But Lord John had been well-acquainted with their sly tricks since his university days and had no trouble recognizing the full-body scratch of a flush pickpocket's fingers reaching through the lining of his trousers. He turned around and swiftly grabbed the woman by the wrist, who yanked her arm away and broke free. Betty ran, dropping her purse all the while. Its contents spilt out onto the ground, but she didn't stop to pick them up. Her bra jingled as she ran, like a starting pistol in a footrace, the sound spurring her on. Without any regard for his reputation and with no malice in his heart, Lord John pitched down the hill, nearly tripping over himself to catch up with the girl. And with that, he was in love.

Chapter 6

The Spencer House

Meanwhile, Otto was on a mission: a mission to find and destroy Earl Francis Ashley's will. The will would give him the details he needed to sort out the Ashley Trust and give Lord John Ashley an equal share of the inheritance by English common law. Otto buttled from time to time at the Spencer House, and so had the necessary access.

He hurried through the streets of London, dressed casually in shirt and slacks and a twinkle in his eye. The house loomed before him, tall and palatial. Made of a pale blue, cream-coloured, and light yellow Victorian design, the house was twisted by age. The windows appeared to be inviting from the outside; were they shut or were they open? On top of it sat stone statues who sorrowfully watched Otto as he entered the front door and padlocked it behind him.

Otto walked around the Spencer House, taking in the splendour of the old building. The structure had been around for centuries, and it was built with elegance and class. The corners and curves of the exterior were carved into pillars and statues, and the interior was greenish-blue and welcoming. The floors were polished oak, which looked smooth to the touch, and a chandelier hung above in the centre of the open room. He noticed the house smelled of old wood, of beeswax and of flowers.

Then, from above the ground floor of this mansion, came a scream. It was high-pitched and shattered the silence of the night. Otto darted upstairs to determine the source of the commotion. He ran at top speed up the spiral staircase to the second level and burst into the master bedroom. It was empty, save for Della Duke, as the servants were all in attendance at the viscount's wedding ball. She was sitting on the edge of the enormous mahogany bed in nothing but a pink silk robe. Earl Francis Ashley lay naked on the bed behind her.

'I've killed him!' she screamed out into the empty mansion, with just her, Otto, and a corpse. Her voice was high-pitched and full of fear. 'I don't understand. He was only just inside me until he stopped breathing. For good!' The man was face-up on the bed, dead. She couldn't believe what she had done. She knew she was a good lover, but she had never killed a man before. It felt like a dream. She knew from books that people died cold and hard, but this man was warm and soft to the touch even though his chest did not rise or fall as her hands pressed against it. A deep sadness came over her as she thought of how much life he must have behind him and how much more this would make him miss. There was no pulse; he couldn't be alive. 'You can't leave me here!' she cried. 'I can't be sent to prison! Oh, please don't tell anyone!' Otto paused and looked again at the earl's lifeless body.

'The will,' he mumbled to himself and inadvertently smiled. 'Listen here, girl. Find his will.' She reluctantly agreed. They searched behind every painting, inside every piano and safe, up and down the staircases, and behind every sputter of candlelight and paintings that looked different from the rest. They found nothing.

They turned their attention to his study. The desk drawers were rifled through again — the papers in them were meaningless — and then the floorboard hiding spots and the high-ceilings hiding spots. Again, nothing was found.

Eventually, Otto reentered the master bedroom, where the body was still lingering. 'It couldn't possibly...' Otto said. He grabbed the warm body's elbow and then pulled to try to lift the corpse off the bed. He doubled his efforts and tried again. The corpse did not move an inch. 'Miss?'

'No. Absolutely not. Concretely no. I am not moving the body,' Della maintained.

'Remember what is at stake,' Otto threatened. He would not lose his leverage over her in this situation, no matter what she thought of him. She begrudgingly lifted his feet, squirming and turning at every micro-movement made by the dead man from their transporting. Otto, after a short rest, lifted the mattress. Underneath were innumerable papers of all sorts: letters, household receipts, and ledgers. None were his will.

'You made me handle a dead body for nothing?' Della cried. She rubbed her temple. Her head throbbed. 'Oh God, what have I done?'

'No, not for nothing,' Otto said, staring into some old manuscripts. 'It's instructions for the lever watch?' Otto looked at the name in the spot marked 'Author:'; it read, 'Fritz Ashley.'

Chapter 7

The Hat and Dress Shoppe

The hat and dress shop moped in the dark, occupied by Betty, Kate, and a sleeping William Acton. A tin sign reading "Fashions From London" clanked when the wind blew through the close-cropped grass. The mighty beech trees tried repeatedly to break in but had little success. As they broke branch after branch they released their leaves; they arced toward the ground like ruddy orange rain. A few of the leaves were caught by Betty's wind chimes and made soft, quiet music that roved through the shop and fell on their heads like a benediction.

'It couldn't be helped,' Betty said. 'He was looking right at me!'

'And imagine the money we've lost!' Kate cried. Betty patted her breast where the rest of the sticky honey still clung to her dress. 'Bugger!' She fished out a few coins — a half-crown, 1 shilling, and 5 pence — which she handed to Kate. 'That's forty-seven pence,' Betty said, disappointed. That was hardly any money at all.

Bert MacAvoy came bursting through the door, a cannonball of a man, and with him, he carried the smell of nicotine and beer. A Beaumont-Adams revolver jutted from his fat hand, a finger twitching on the trigger. A sneer twisted his mouth into an ugly line.

'Where's the ratbag? William! I know you're in here!' MacAvoy shouted toward the back of the house. He leapt into the entryway, his gun pointed like a compass at the sisters. Frightened, confused, and shaking, they cowered against each other, trying to shield themselves from the chaos.

A branch plummeted from behind in a wide arc, its weight pulling its thick trunk downward. Its tip struck the man across the back of his head, and he tumbled forward. Blood splattered out from the man's nose and landed in a small glass bowl inhabited by goldfish. The fish swam frantically around the bowl until their orange bodies were tinged red with blood and they floated away on their backs and died. Blood ran from the gash on MacAvoy's scalp. The large drop of blood dripped from his hair, bounced from his eyebrow and nose, and rubbed into his lips. It ran in streams down his face, joining the leaves and twigs that littered his ugly features.

There stood Lord John Ashley, branch in hand, with a look of solemn authority on his face. He was staring intensely at Betty and Kate, who were standing in front of him. The silence was a low, pulsing roar. It felt like a wave of heat, a storm cloud ready to open up and drown the village in torrential rains and possums that could be sold for half a cow. It felt like a hurricane, building above the hills and coming to rest at the edge of town. The silence was heavy, tangible enough to be lifted up, filled with the promise of breaking point. It was as if a million people had suddenly fallen silent all at once at this one moment, promising that the world would never be the same. Neither Lord John nor Betty knew the etiquette for this situation. Should she thank him? Should he ask if they were okay?

'Blimey, what was that noise,' a drunk William Acton slurred, walking into the foyer. He laid his eyes upon Lord John and the bloody body beneath him until the pain in his head and his body forced him to collapse. 'Ow!' he said. 'That's me head.'

The miniature bell jingled just beside the door as another customer entered the shop. Lord John looked up at two of his dearest friends: Otto Schenk and Della Duke. The two of them were huffing and puffing and were out of breath by the time they reached the counter. Otto had his right arm slung around Della's shoulder for support as she half-dragged and half-carried him across the store. John jumped to his feet and rushed to their aid. 'Otto! Della!' John exclaimed. 'What happened?!'

'My lord,' Otto barely managed to get out. Lord John's face drooped like a sad basset hound, Bert MacAvoy rested looking as if to soon be laid in a coffin, William Acton huffed, Otto Schenk puffed, Betty Acton opened her mouth to an 'O' but closed it with a snap when it registered that Katie Acton was wailing, while Della Duke screamed, at the sight of the second and third collapsed bodies she had seen tonight.

'Carry the body to the backroom,' Lord John demanded, seriously. 'And stop with that screaming. You'll get us all in trouble.' He took MacAvoy's legs and Otto took his arms, all of which still pulsating. Then they did the same with Acton. Blood dripped arbitrarily onto peacock hats and laced dresses. They laid the men on the bed together. Della tried to make a run for it, her pink silk robe flapping in the wind behind her, and Betty quickly grabbed her wrist, halting her escape. The women stood face-to-face, waiting for the other to make a move. Della was a half-head and more slender than Betty.

'You're stuck with us now,' Betty snapped, her eyes flashing; her thin face turned white so that her stooped nose and flared nostrils stood out. She locked the doors from the inside and then placed herself with deliberate casualness by the front door, while Della reluctantly stationed herself in the foyer.

'We've been searching high and low all over London for you.' Otto, still out of breath, said to Lord John. 'We found something.'

'The will?'

'Better.' He lifted the papers to Lord John's chest, who took a completely quiet and undisturbed look.

'A lever watch manual?' Lord John questioned. 'What's this got to do with anything?' He peered toward the upper right corner of the first paper; etched in was the name, Fritz Ashley.

His finger slowly traced each letter of his father's name. With each stroke he remembered sitting at his father's knee, learning to write. The rigid, angular letters of their language were awkward to form. He had never figured out how to control the pen as well as his peers and brothers. His beautiful script was always slower and woefully off-centre, just like his father's.

Chapter 8

Home

'And that's the story. He threatened to expose MacAvoy to the public but was compensated for it and given some money for his debts. He was then also given some additional money — £10,000 — as sort of thanks for keeping quiet about it but exposed MacAvoy anyways, who then lost his degree from Oxford and had to work —as luck would have it — as a butler!'

A young man and woman — brother and sister about 18 and 21 — were curled up on a couch listening to their mother tell the story. Their bodies were tight against one another, back to back and knee to knee, like two peas in a pod. They were identical except for the colour of their eyes: the man's was blue like the sky and the woman's more of an brownish colour. Eyes locked on the storyteller, they smiled softly at the funny parts and winced with concern at the scary parts.

'Papa, is this true?' the daughter asked, turning her focus to her father.

'All of it.'

'You're telling us Christian Aunt Della was once a whore?' asked the brother, with a coffee-coloured moustache like his father.

'And rich Uncle Otto was once a butler?' asked the daughter, whose black curls scattered haphazardly on the sofa.

'Indeed,' the mother said.

'And what became of grandfather's hat and dress shop?'

Sitting between an apothecary and K. Acton's Bakery, the family's house was situated on a slight slope and saturated with the familiar smell of cedarwood, but every time the door swung open, bringing in a gust of English summer air and the scent of hollyhocks from a nearby garden, the warm wind roared in with them. The rustling of leaves in the wind drowned out the sound of carriages and the rumble of horseless carriages on asphalt streets below. The weathervanes atop the structure moved back and forth like little soldiers in their cages for a moment, for they did not like being confined. Wind blew through the great beech trees, prompting their branches to reach toward the windows that separated them from the inside. They touched the glass but did nothing more, for the glass was strong and would not let them in.

THE END.

Printed in Great Britain
by Amazon